Dear mouse friends,
Welcome to the world of

Geronimo Stilton

THE RODENT'S GAZETTE
EDITORIAL STAFF

Geronimo Stilton
A learned and brainy
mouse; editor of
The Rodent's Gazette

Thea Stilton
Geronimo's sister and
special correspondent at
The Rodent's Gazette

Trap Stilton
An awful joker;
Geronimo's cousin and
owner of the store
Cheap Junk for Less

Benjamin Stilton
A sweet and loving
nine-year-old mouse;
Geronimo's favorite
nephew

Geronimo Stilton

THE SUPER SCAM

Scholastic Inc.

New York   Toronto   London   Auckland
Sydney   Mexico City   New Delhi   Hong Kong

ISBN 978-0-545-56016-0

Based on an original idea by Elisabetta Dami.
www.geronimostilton.com

Published by Scholastic Inc., 557 Broadway, New York, NY 10012.
SCHOLASTIC and associated logos are trademarks and/or registered trademarks of Scholastic Inc.

Stilton is the name of a famous English cheese. It is a registered trademark of the Stilton Cheese Makers' Association. For more information, go to www.stiltoncheese.com.

Text by Geronimo Stilton
Original title *Una truffa coi baffi*
Cover by Giuseppe Ferrario
Illustrations by Paolo De Capite (pencils and ink) and Anna Ziche (color)
Graphics by Michela Battaglin

Special thanks to Kathryn Cristaldi
Translated by Julia Heim
Interior design by Becky James

Fingerprint on cover and page i © NREY/Shutterstock

First Printing, November 2012
Reprinted by Scholastic Malaysia, operating under Grolier (Malaysia) Sdn. Bhd., November 2012
Printed in Malaysia

ONE LONG WEEK

It was a chilly evening in November. I was at home, sprawled out on my favorite pawchair in front of a cozy fire. It had been one *LONG* week. I had been running my tail off at the newspaper.

Oops! Excuse me — I always forget to introduce myself. My name is Stilton, *Geronimo Stilton*. I run *The Rodent's Gazette*, the most famouse newspaper on Mouse Island.

Anyway, where was I? Oh, yes, I was relaxing at home with a **STEAMING** cup of chamomile tea in my left paw and a pawful of my favorite chocolate **Cheesy Chews** in my right.

Soothing classical music filled the room. I was listening to the one and only **Mozart**. What a musical genius! I sighed happily.

I had just closed my eyes and put my paws up on my pawrest when all of a sudden . . . DING DONG!

My doorbell rang.

I jumped a foot, **flinging** my tea into the air.

So much for a relaxing night!

URGENT LETTER FOR MR. GERONIMO STILTON

I shuffled to my front door.

"Who is it?" I squeaked nervously. It was after ten p.m. Who would be ringing my doorbell so late?

"Mail!" yelled a high-pitched voice on the other side.

Mail? In the middle of the night?

"URGENT letter for Mr. Geronimo Stilton. Can you please open the door? I need your signature," the voice continued.

I opened the door, signed a form, then returned to my pawchair to read the letter. It said:

BUY-O-RAMA SUPERSTORE

Dear Customer,

You are cordially invited to the grand opening of Squeakman's Buy-O-Rama Superstore this Sunday at our fabumouse New Mouse City location. Every guest will receive free wireless Squeakman's Super Headphones! See you there!

Cheesily yours,

Cyril Squeakman

Scratch the cheese symbol next to this message. You could be the lucky winner of a cheese-scented mountain bike!

If it's at Squeakman's, you gotta have it!

Cyril Squeakman

I was thinking about what I would do with a cheese-scented mountain bike (I'm not a great biker) when the phone **rang**.

RRRIIIIIINNNNNGGGG!!!

Once again I jumped a foot, this time **flinging** the letter in the air.

So much for a relaxing night!

Aaaahhhhh!

HELLO! HELLO! HELLO!

As soon as I picked up the phone, a mouse began *squeaking* my ear off.

"HELLO! HELLO! HELLO! I'm Cindy from Squeakman's Buy-O-Rama Superstore and do I have some great news for you!" she gushed. "You are the lucky winner of a FREE gift card to use at our new store!

CONGRATULATIONS!

Just present the card and you'll receive

a **FREE** pair of Squeakman's super-
stretchy suspenders!"

I tried to explain that I prefer wearing
a **BELT**, but she cut me off.

MOLDY MOZZARELLA, that mouse could
squeak! She insisted that I write down

a **Secret code** that would allow me to collect my prize.

But while trying to get a notepad, I *tripped* on the phone cord and fell flat on my snout!

KABOOM!

Forget the suspenders — I might need a pair of crutches! I thought as Cindy rattled off my **Secret code**. Then she chirped good-bye and **hung up** before I had a chance to write it down.

"Thanks," I murmured, still lying on the floor.

A few seconds later the phone rang again.

So much for a RELAXING night!

CAN WE GO?

I sighed and picked up the phone.

"Stilton residence," I answered, looking wistfully at my **cozy** pawchair.

"Hi, Uncle!" a little voice squeaked.

I cheered up instantly. It was my dear nephew **BENJAMIN**.

I would do anything for him! So when he asked me if I would take him to the opening, I said **yes** without even thinking.

Hi, Uncle!

Then I realized I had **no idea** what opening he was talking about.

"The grand opening of **SBS**, of course!" he explained.

"SBS?" I mumbled.

"**SQUEAKMAN'S BUY-O-RAMA SUPERSTORE!** Didn't you see the commercial on TV? They're giving away **FREE** wireless Squeakman's Super Headphones! Can we go?" he pleaded.

First I turned as yellow as Swiss cheese . . .

1

2

. . . then as red as a tomato . . .

... then as brown as a bar of milk chocolate.

3

If there's one thing I hate, it's shopping! And I especially hate those ginormouse shopping centers — they're usually filled with teenage **MALL RATS**. But I would rather RIP out all my whiskers than disappoint my nephew.

So I said, "Of course, we can go! In fact, we'll be the *first* ones to get there!"

JUST A FEW MORE PAWSTEPS!

What a bad idea!

That Sunday, *everyone* else in New Mouse City also went to the **GRAND OPENING** of *SBS*. As soon as we got in the car, we were stuck in a **HUGE** traffic jam!

The whole time, the face of Cyril Squeakman **grinned** down at us from billboards on the side of the road.

IT WAS A REALLY REALLY LONG TRIP . . .

TWO HOURS AND FIFTEEN MINUTES to reach the parking lot!

FORTY-FIVE MINUTES to drive around the whole parking lot without finding a spot!

HALF AN HOUR to squeeze in between two SUVs in another parking lot five miles away! (Parking lot Z, row 899!)

FIFTEEN MINUTES to get out of the car — using the window!

. . . BUT WE FINALLY ARRIVED!

Well, I *thought* we had arrived. Until I realized that we had to cross **ALL** the parking lots and follow a **tON** of signs to get there:

> **THIS WAY TO SQUEAKMAN'S!**

> **JUST A FEW MORE PAWSTEPS!**

> **YOU'RE ALMOST THERE!**

What a workout! I was *EXHAUSTED*! Did I mention I'm not the most athletic mouse on the block?

"Come on, Uncle. You can do it!" Benjamin encouraged me. I tried to

smile, but by the time I arrived at the entrance to Squeakman's Buy-O-Rama Superstore, I was a **wreck**. My heart was **POUNDING** and my tongue was dangling out of my mouth.

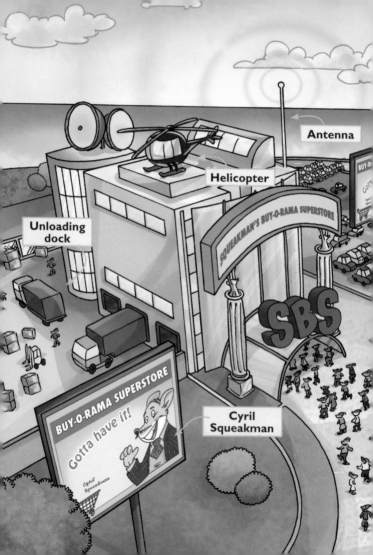

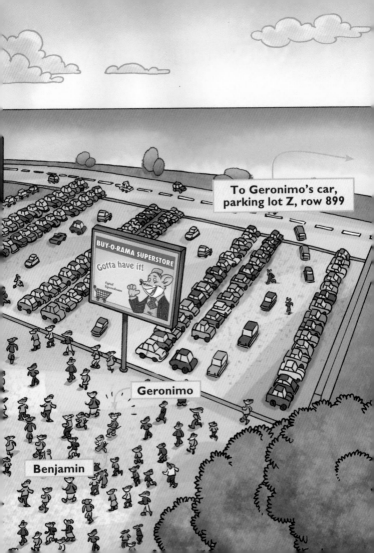

A LONG LINE OF MICE

When I stopped
panting, I looked
around. The first
thing I noticed was
a helicopter
parked on the roof. Then I saw
a really TALL antenna. Strange.

A LONG line of mice stood in
front of a big flashing sign that read
FREE WIRELESS SQUEAKMAN'S SUPER
HEADPHONES!

Benjamin and I got in line with
everyone else. While I was waiting, I

tried not to **SCREAM**. It wasn't easy because:

MY PAW GOT STEPPED ON 36 TIMES!

I GOT ELBOWED IN THE STOMACH 14 TIMES!

A VERY HEAVY MOUSE FELL ASLEEP ON MY SHOULDER!

After forty-five minutes, we FiNALLY arrived at the counter, where **Cyril Squeakman** himself waited on us with a big PHONY smile.

Cyril Squeakman

CLUE 1

What strange thing do you notice on the roof of Squeakman's store?

CYRIL SQUEAKMAN

"Mr. Stilton! What a pleasure!" he bellowed, **crushing** my paw in his.

I blinked. "Do we know each other?" I asked, wincing. My paw was **throbbing**. Where was a nice bucket of **ice** when you needed one?

"Oh, don't be shy, Stilton! I'm a big fan! *The Rodent's Gazette* . . . your many books . . . I've read them all!" he declared. His smile was so bright it hurt my eyes. "And who is this **adorable** young mouse?" he asked, patting Benjamin on the back.

Nice to meet you, Benny!

"This is my nephew Benjamin," I replied.

"Nice to meet you, Benny!" he said in his **TOO-LOUD** voice.

Then he handed us each a headset.

"Here are your **FREE** gifts! Two incredible sets of **Squeakman's Super Headphones**. Put them on! They will help you select our products. And you use this button for your **SQUEAKMAN'S SUPER CART**. Happy shopping, Stiltons!" he cried, crushing my paw once more.

I wondered if I would ever be able to write with it again.

GOTTA HAVE IT!

Benjamin put on his headset and took off into the crowd.

"Wait for me!" I called, grabbing a shopping cart.

But he couldn't hear me.

I sighed and put on my headset. I was definitely not in the **MOOD** to shop, but what else could I do?

The minute I put on the headset, happy music filled my ears. Suddenly, I had the urge to DANCE!

And when I glanced up, I realized everyone else was Dancing, too!

I tried to resist the temptation to dance, but it was practically impossible. (HOW STRANGE — I don't even like dancing!)

I found myself JUMPING around with my headset on. I felt so happy!

I looked at the shelves and started to grab everything in my reach.

I got . . .

5 pounds of Swiss cheese,

2 Squeakman's alarm clock radios,

10 containers of Squeakman's shower gel,

13 baseball hats that said "I love SBS!"

1 Squeakman's Multi-tasker Smoothie Machine with a built-in fur dryer, and

7 tubes of fur-quenching aloe butter!

Benjamin was doing the same thing.

He had put in the cart:

1 enormouse teddy bear,
7 Squeak-Station video games,
2 pairs of swim fins,
5 boxes of Squeakman's chocolates,
400 inflatable balloons,
12 blue SBS bouncy balls, and
1 giant motorized car shaped like an elephant!

As I shopped, I sang out, "**Gotta have it!**" I was so happy!

CLUE 2

Why do Geronimo and Benjamin suddenly feel so happy and have a strange desire to dance?

POP! POP! POP!

Soon I was pushing such a **FULL** cart that I couldn't even see where I was going. I ended up **CRASHING** into another Squeakman's Super Cart **JAM-PACKED** with items. It was being pushed by a large mouse.

She was moving so *fast* she rolled right over me and kept on going. I hit the ground with a **thud** that sent my headset flying. Then I heard a sound like a thousand soap bubbles popping.

When the sound stopped, I looked around in confusion. . . .

Why was everyone dancing and singing, "**Gotta have it!**"?

Even my nephew Benjamin was kicking up his paws and singing. I felt like I was stuck in the middle of a **Gotta have it!** music video!

How **STRANGE**!

Just then a security mouse in  dark glasses approached me. He was dressed in black and had a small microphone in front of his mouth.

"Are you **okay**, sir?" he asked me.

"Well . . . I . . . ," I began.

But he cut me off.

"Let me help you," he said. Then he

picked up everything and
put it back in my cart.

"Th-th-thank you,"
I stammered. The dark
glasses were so **CREEPY**. Why wear
them inside? I thought about asking him,
but instead I said, "Why is
everyone **singing** and
DANCING?"

The security mouse ignored me.
He just **JAMMED** my headset back
onto my head. Then he squeaked
into his microphone:
**"DANGER AVERTED.
SITUATION UNDER CONTROL."**

I started to **FROWN**, but then I heard the music coming from my headset. I was happy again!

Before long I met up with Benjamin at **REGISTER NUMBER 320**.

CLUE 3

Why did the security mouse say "danger averted" into his microphone?

DID YOU GO SHOPPING?

I spent a **TON** of money without batting a whisker — we needed **44** shopping bags for all the things we bought! Plus, I received my free Squeakman's super-**stretchy** suspenders even though I didn't have the **Secret code**.

I was so happy. It took me forever to get everything packed into the car, but I never stopped smiling. Finally, we took off, SINGING at the tops of our lungs along with the music on our headsets: "Gotta have it!"

At home, we unloaded our purchases in the living room. Then the MUSIC in my headset turned off by itself. Again I heard a sound like a thousand soap bubbles popping.

POP! POP! POP! POP!

I looked around the room at all the useless JUNK I had bought. Suddenly, I began to feel very unhappy.

Meanwhile, Benjamin was still smiling, staring into space, and humming along with his headphones. What was happening? Why did the music have this STRANGE effect?

I pulled the headset off Benjamin's head. After a few minutes, he stared at me, looking totally confused, and said, "What is all this stuff, Uncle? Did you go shopping?"

HE DIDN'T REMEMBER A THING!

By now, I was feeling totally confused myself. Why would I go shopping? I hate shopping! Was it all a bad dream?

I was so exhausted I decided to sleep on it.

WHAT KIND OF
PRODUCT WAS THIS?

The next day at six in the morning, the two Squeakman's alarm clock radios began **SQUEAKING** so loud I leaped out of bed like a **HIGH-JUMP** champion!

GOOD MORNING FROM SQUEAKMAN'S BUY-O-RAMA SUPERSTORE! IF IT'S AT SQUEAKMAN'S, YOU **GOTTA** HAVE IT!

Suddenly, I remembered shopping at Squeakman's and all the STUFF Benjamin and I had bought. I took a shower with my new Squeakman's shower gel, and within two minutes I was covered in itchy red bumps. What kind of product was this?

I thought I would get rid of them with a little Squeakman's aloe butter, but the bumps just turned GREEN and the itching got WORSE!

What kind of product was this?

Argh!

Help!

Yuck!

Then I tried to make myself a mozzarella and banana-kiwi milkshake with my new Squeakman's Multi-tasker Smoothie Machine with built-in fur dryer. But when I turned on the blender, the fur dryer kicked on, too, spewing shake all over my head and the kitchen ceiling. What kind of product was this?

Oops!

I cleaned myself up and tried on my new Squeakman's super-stretchy suspenders. But they stretched so much my pants fell to the floor. What kind of product was this?

Hmph!

Finally, I opened up a box of Squeakman's chocolates. **HOW** can you mess up chocolate? But after only one nibble, my teeth were completely stuck together!

I promised myself I would never set foot in that junk-filled **SUPERSTORE** ever again! I headed out to my office, **fuming**.

Just then I heard a mother shrieking because a wheel had **rolled** off her new Squeakman's baby stroller.

Next I spotted two little mice on their way to school with new Squeakman's  backpacks that had come *unstitched*, as well as a jogger who had lost a sole off one of his new Squeakman's **sneakers**. **Holey cheese!** I thought. *Squeakman is ripping everybody off! Someone should turn that rotten fur ball in!* I reached the office, determined to write a **NASTY** article about him in my paper. I had already thought of the headline:

WHAT WAS GOING ON?

I was heading for my desk when I realized there was something strange about the office. All my coworkers were dancing around wearing Squeakman's Super Headphones. "**Gotta have it! Gotta have it!**" they sang happily.

I grabbed one of the new editors, Katie Cheeseheart, and squeaked, "What's going on?"

She looked at me with a grin. In addition to her headset, she was also wearing a T-shirt that said "I ♥ SBS"!

I gulped. Something told me I already knew the answer.

Katie lifted up her headset. "We're listening to the Squeakman's station. The music's SO catchy! Put on your headset!" she crooned, dancing away.

Double gulp. I ran to my desk.

A few minutes later, Patty Plumprat appeared at my **office** door. She held up the first proof of the newspaper.

"Look, Mr. Stilton. Isn't this great?" she asked.

When I saw it, I nearly **HIT** the ceiling. The whole last page was an ad for Squeakman's!

In the ad, Cyril wore his phony grin by a slogan that read "**Gotta have it!**"

"Who approved this?" I asked Patty, my head **POUNDING**.

"Your sister did, Mr. Stilton," Patty answered.

I called Thea. She wasn't in. "You have reached the voice mail of Thea Stilton," her message squeaked. "Sorry you missed me. I'm at the **SBS SUPER SALE**. Half price off all Squeakman's in-line skates, skateboards, and accessories! **Gotta have it!**"

I groaned. **What was going on?**

PUT ME ON!

I left the office and **ran** home.

I had to figure out why **every mouse** I knew was dying to shop at Squeakman's. It didn't make sense. New Mouse City had a lot of malls whose products were much better quality than Squeakman's.

I made myself a nice cup of tea and stared at my **Squeakman's Super Headphones**. They were turned off, or at least it seemed that way.

All of a sudden a **BUZZ** started coming out of the headset! A voice commanded, "**PUT ME ON! PUT ME ON!**" over and over.

Before I could stop myself, I reached for the headset. I felt like I had **no choice**. I had to put it on! But before I could, the voice stopped.

Then it started up again. "**PUT ME ON . . . BZZZZ!**"

Finally, the headset turned off for good. It was **BROKEN**.

Just like before, I heard the sound of a thousand bubbles popping.

POP! POP! POP!

Suddenly, I clapped my paw to my head. "**That's it!**" I squeaked. At last,

I understood exactly what was going on!

But before I could do anything, the doorbell rang.

It was my nephew Benjamin and his friend Bugsy Wugsy. They were both happily wearing their headsets.

"Hi, Uncle! Can we go **back**?" Benjamin exclaimed.

"Go back . . . **where**?" I asked, already knowing the answer.

Bugsy rolled her eyes. "Where else, Uncle G? To Squeakman's!" she shouted.

CLUE 4

What did Geronimo finally understand?

You'd Better Lie Down

I pulled Benjamin and Bugsy inside. Then I removed their **headphones**.

"Wait . . . ," Bugsy protested.

"What's going on, Uncle?" Benjamin asked, looking confused.

I tried to explain. "I think there is something **strange** about those **headphones**," I said. "For some reason, whenever anyone puts them on, they want to go **SHOPPING** at Squeakman's."

Benjamin scratched his head. "But the headphones only play **music**," he mumbled.

"Yeah," agreed Bugsy. "Music can't convince you to go shopping, Uncle G. Maybe you'd better lie down. You're sounding a little CUCKOO. Did you get hit on the head recently? How many WHISKERS do I have?"

Bugsy stuck her snout in my face. I ignored her.

"I'm telling you, the headphones convince you to do things. Before you got here, mine started squeaking, 'PUT ME ON!' Then they broke," I insisted.

Bugsy rolled her eyes. Benjamin coughed.

Why didn't they believe me?

SUBLIMINAL SOUND
WAVES

Then I got an idea. I would ask my friend
the famouse scientist **Professor Paws Von
Volt** what he thought.

It took the professor less than ten
minutes to solve the mystery.

"What you are describing, Geronimo,
is something called *subliminal sound
waves*," he said. "They are sound waves
that have the power to hypnotize.
Anyone who listens to them will do
whatever they are instructed to do."

"Like go shopping for JUNK at
Squeakman's superstore?" I said.

The professor nodded. "And with a powerful antenna, these **waves** could be spread miles away," he added.

I blinked, picturing the **HUMONGOUS** antenna we had spotted on top of SBS.

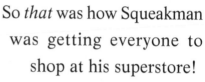

So *that* was how Squeakman was getting everyone to shop at his superstore!

"That place is no **SUPERSTORE**!" Bugsy squeaked. "It's a **super scam**!"

"You can say that again!" I agreed.

"That place is no **SUPERSTORE**! It's

a **super scam**!"
Bugsy repeated.

Benjamin
giggled. Then
he grabbed my paw.
"Remember when you
RAN into that mouse with
your cart, and your headset
fell off? It must have
broken then," he guessed.

I shook my head, remembering. It
was a good thing that had happened.
Otherwise we might never have solved
the **mystery**. For once, my clumsiness
had paid off!

"**That's it!** I'm bringing these

headphones to the police. They'll arrest that **rotten** swindler Cyril Squeakman! It's time he stopped ripping off everyone in New Mouse City!" I said.

I was about to run to the police station when Benjamin and Bugsy stopped me.

"Wait, Uncle G. We've got a better idea. We just need the professor's help with these," Bugsy said, holding up the headphones.

CLUE 5

What do Benjamin and Bugsy want to do with the headphones?

WE WANT OUR MONEY BACK!

The professor knew what Benjamin and **BUGSY** wanted to do with the headphones — reprogram them! He got right to work.

The next morning we met at my house, then headed to **SQUEAKMAN'S**. I couldn't wait to get to the superstore — but for a different reason this time!

As soon as we arrived,

I stared up at the helicopter and the **EXTRA-LONG** antenna on the roof. I could see exactly where those sound waves were transmitted!

Just like last time, **SBS** was mobbed with mice. But today nobody looked happy. Nobody was singing or dancing or wearing headphones. In fact, everyone looked **FURIOUS**. And the line at the complaint counter was two miles **long**!

"This cat-fur coat has two **holes** in the armpits!" yelled the large mouse who had rolled her cart over me before.

"This thermal blanket shoots out **sparks**! It set my bed on fire!" yelled an old rodent with a cane.

"This bottle **leaks**! It soaked my precious mouselet!" yelled a mother mouse.

"WE WANT OUR MONEY BACK!" yelled everybody.

A mouse dressed in black tried to CALM everyone down. It didn't work.

The protests grew LOUDER.

"Where's Squeakman?" someone shouted.

"Yeah, where's the CROOK?" yelled someone else.

But Cyril Squeakman was nowhere in sight.

"Looks like everyone got the **new message** through their headphones, Professor," Benjamin said with a grin.

"**Gotta return it! Gotta return it!**" sang Bugsy, collapsing in a fit of giggles.

I smiled happily. It felt good to put **SQUEAKMAN THE SWINDLER** out of business.

As we returned to the car, we spotted the black helicopter.

Speaking of Squeakman . . .

GOOD RIDDANCE TO SQUEAKMAN!

"Look, Uncle!" shouted Benjamin. "It's Cyril Squeakman! He's **sneaking** away!"

I watched as the helicopter lifted off, leaving the superstore far behind. I thought about calling the police, but when I looked at the crowd of rodents **smiling**, I decided everything would be okay as it was.

"**Good riddance** to Squeakman!" everyone cheered.

The next day I ran an article on the front page of *The Rodent's Gazette* with the headline "**Squeakman's Shuts**

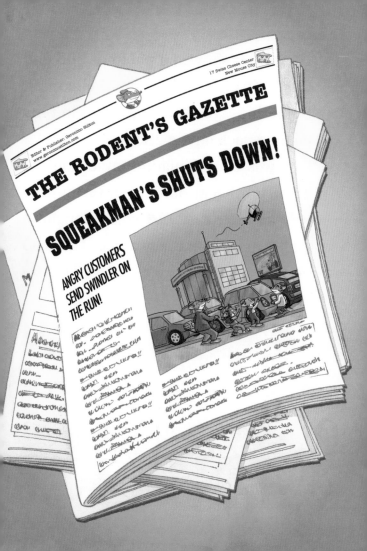

Down!" It showed a photo of SBS and Cyril *FLYING* off in his helicopter. Something told me he wouldn't be coming back anytime soon.

I was congratulating myself on the great job I had done discovering this **SUPERSTORE SCAM** when Benjamin and Bugsy flew into my office. They had headphones on and were **JUMPING** around.

"Uncle G, will you take us to the new toy store downtown? They're giving away free SUPERMOUSE action figures!" they pleaded.

Oh, no! Not again! I cringed. But a minute later Benjamin and Bugsy both collapsed into a fit of giggles.

"Just joking!" they squeaked, hugging me.

I grinned. I don't need a SUPERMOUSE action figure to know that I, Geronimo Stilton, am **SUPER**-lucky to have such wonderful family and friends!

1 **What strange thing do you notice on the roof of Squeakman's superstore?**

The roof has an enormouse antenna on it.

2 **Why do Geronimo and Benjamin suddenly feel so happy and have a strange desire to dance?**

Because of the music from their headphones.

3 **Why did the security mouse say "danger averted" into his microphone?**

Because he got the headphones back on Geronimo's head before Geronimo noticed anything fishy.

4 **What did Geronimo finally understand?**

That his headphones were what had made him want to dance and go shopping.

5 **What do Benjamin and Bugsy want to do with the headphones?**

They want to change the message played on the headphones so that mice will want to return their broken merchandise.

HOW MANY QUESTIONS DID YOU ANSWER CORRECTLY?

ALL 5 CORRECT: You are a
SUPER-SQUEAKY INVESTIGATOR!

FROM 2 TO 4 CORRECT: You are a
SUPER INVESTIGATOR! You'll get
that added squeak soon!

LESS THAN 2 CORRECT: You are
a GOOD INVESTIGATOR! Keep
practicing to get super-squeaky!

Farewell until the next mystery!

Geronimo Stilton

Check out all my
mini mysteries!

Don't miss any of my other fabumouse adventures!

#1 Lost Treasure of the Emerald Eye

#2 The Curse of the Cheese Pyramid

#3 Cat and Mouse in a Haunted House

#4 I'm Too Fond of My Fur!

#5 Four Mice Deep in the Jungle

#6 Paws Off, Cheddarface!

#7 Red Pizzas for a Blue Count

#8 Attack of the Bandit Cats

#9 A Fabumouse Vacation for Geronimo

#10 All Because of a Cup of Coffee

#11 It's Halloween, You 'Fraidy Mouse!

#12 Merry Christmas, Geronimo!

#13 The Phantom of the Subway

#14 The Temple of the Ruby of Fire

#15 The Mona Mousa Code

#16 A Cheese-Colored Camper

#17 Watch Your Whiskers, Stilton!

#18 Shipwreck on the Pirate Islands

#19 My Name Is
Stilton, Geronimo
Stilton

#20 Surf's Up,
Geronimo!

#21 The Wild,
Wild West

#22 The Secret
of Cacklefur
Castle

A Christmas Tale

#23 Valentine's
Day Disaster

#24 Field Trip to
Niagara Falls

#25 The Search
for Sunken
Treasure

#26 The Mummy
with No Name

#27 The
Christmas Toy
Factory

#28 Wedding
Crasher

#29 Down and
Out Down Under

#30 The Mouse
Island Marathon

#31 The
Mysterious
Cheese Thief

Christmas
Catastrophe

#32 Valley of the
Giant Skeletons

#33 Geronimo
and the Gold
Medal Mystery

#34 Geronimo
Stilton, Secret
Agent

#35 A Very
Merry Christmas

#36 Geronimo's
Valentine

#37 The Race Across America

#38 A Fabumouse School Adventure

#39 Singing Sensation

#40 The Karate Mouse

#41 Mighty Mount Kilimanjaro

#42 The Peculiar Pumpkin Thief

#43 I'm Not a Supermouse!

#44 The Giant Diamond Robbery

#45 Save the White Whale!

#46 The Haunted Castle

#47 Run for the Hills, Geronimo!

#48 The Mystery in Venice

#49 The Way of the Samurai

#50 This Hotel Is Haunted!

#51 The Enormouse Pearl Heist

Don't miss these very special editions!

THE KINGDOM OF FANTASY

THE QUEST FOR PARADISE: THE RETURN TO THE KINGDOM OF FANTASY

THE AMAZING VOYAGE: THE THIRD ADVENTURE IN THE KINGDOM OF FANTASY

THE DRAGON PROPHECY: THE FOURTH ADVENTURE IN THE KINGDOM OF FANTASY

ABOUT THE AUTHOR

 Born in New Mouse City, Mouse Island, **GERONIMO STILTON** is Rattus Emeritus of Mousomorphic Literature and of Neo-Ratonic Comparative Philosophy. For the past twenty years, he has been running *The Rodent's Gazette*, New Mouse City's most widely read daily newspaper.

Stilton was awarded the Ratitzer Prize for his scoops on *The Curse of the Cheese Pyramid* and *The Search for Sunken Treasure*. He has also received the Andersen 2000 Prize for Personality of the Year. One of his bestsellers won the 2002 eBook Award for world's best ratlings' electronic book. His works have been published all over the globe.

In his spare time, Mr. Stilton collects antique cheese rinds and plays golf. But what he most enjoys is telling stories to his nephew Benjamin.

1. Main entrance
2. Printing presses (where the books and newspaper are printed)
3. Accounts department
4. Editorial room (where the editors, illustrators, and designers work)
5. Geronimo Stilton's office
6. Helicopter landing pad

THE RODENT'S GAZETTE

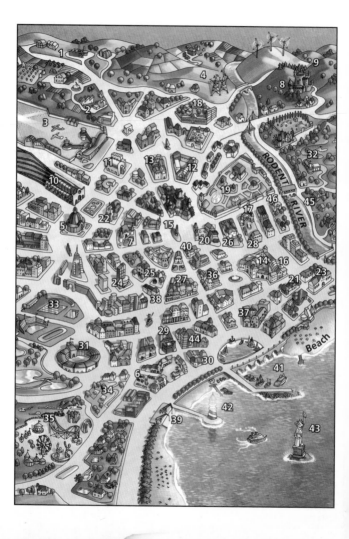

Map of New Mouse City

Brigand's Isle

This way to the Rodent Straits

Tomcat Island

Pirate Ship of Cats

Hamster Islands

Coral Reefs

Blue Dolphin Bay

This way to the Mousific Ocean

Stray Cat Harbor

Cat's Claw Bay

Panther Archipelago

Swissville

Cheddarton

Mouseport

This way to the Ratlantic Ocean

San Mouscisco

New Mouse City

Mousefort Beach

Furflung Island

This way to the Sea of Mice

N
W   E
S

MOUSE ISLAND

1
2
3
4
5
6
7
8
9
10
11
12
13
14
15
16
17
18
19
20
21
22
23
24
25
26
27
28
29
30
31
32
33
34
35
36
37

Map of Mouse Island

1. Big Ice Lake
2. Frozen Fur Peak
3. Slipperyslopes Glacier
4. Coldcreeps Peak
5. Ratzikistan
6. Transratania
7. Mount Vamp
8. Roastedrat Volcano
9. Brimstone Lake
10. Poopedcat Pass
11. Stinko Peak
12. Dark Forest
13. Vain Vampires Valley
14. Goose Bumps Gorge
15. The Shadow Line Pass
16. Penny Pincher Castle
17. Nature Reserve Park
18. Las Ratayas Marinas
19. Fossil Forest
20. Lake Lake
21. Lake Lakelake
22. Lake Lakelakelake
23. Cheddar Crag
24. Cannycat Castle
25. Valley of the Giant Sequoia
26. Cheddar Springs
27. Sulfurous Swamp
28. Old Reliable Geyser
29. Vole Vale
30. Ravingrat Ravine
31. Gnat Marshes
32. Munster Highlands
33. Mousehara Desert
34. Oasis of the Sweaty Camel
35. Cabbagehead Hill
36. Rattytrap Jungle
37. Rio Mosquito

Dear mouse friends,
Thanks for reading, and farewell
until the next mystery!

Geronimo Stilton